D1308777

For my parents

First published in the United States by
Ideals Publishing Corporation
Nashville, Tennessee 37214

Created and produced by
The Templar Company plc
Dorking, Surrey, England

Text and illustrations copyright © 1990 by
The Templar Company plc
All rights reserved. No part of this publication may be
reproduced or transmitted in any form or by any means,
electronic or mechanical, including photocopying, recording,
or any information storage and retrieval system, without
permission in writing from the publisher.

Printed and bound in Italy

Library of Congress Cataloging-in-Publication Data

Ward, Helen, 1962-
The moonrat and the white turtle / written and illustrated by
Helen Ward.
p.   cm.
Summary: Moonrat, the leader of a band of pirate rats, plots
to steal the moon from the sky and add it to his treasure hoard.
ISBN 0-8249-8467-6
[1. Pirates—Fiction.   2. Rats—Fiction.   3. Moon—Fiction.
4. Turtles—Fiction.]   I. Title.
PZ7.W2124Mo   1990
[E]—dc20
90-33363
CIP
AC

The

MOONRAT

and the White Turtle

Written and illustrated by

Helen Ward

IDEALS CHILDREN'S BOOKS

O nce upon a time under a distant blue sky, in a distant blue ocean, where the land was fractured into countless islands, there lived . . . pirates!

Chief and most greedy of them all was the dreaded Moonrat. With a motley band of brigands and his ship, the *Sea Serpent*, he hunted the sea routes for rich merchant vessels. And when he found them, he pounded them with cannon fire and, with cutlass drawn, ransacked their holds for treasure. The nightmares of seamen everywhere were full of the Moonrat's fearsome face.

After each successful raid, the pirates landed their plunder at a secret hideout, an island of two rocky towers with a small, white beach and a hidden harbor in between. At the very top of one cliff, carved into the rock itself, stood an ancient and long-deserted palace, overgrown with tangled trees and wild, exotic flowers.

Here the pirates lived over and under and next to their booty. The whole rocky pinnacle was riddled with corridors and passageways and stony vaults. Even the deepest and darkest rooms were stuffed to the ceilings with plunder.

There were gold and silver, crystal and glass, and jewels of all colors and designs. They glinted in the lamplight and were reflected in the pirates' watchful eyes. Dusty paintings and gold-framed mirrors, silks, and tapestries were all covered in cobwebs. There were caverns of cutlasses, swords, and spears, where plumed helmets rested on brilliant shields and plated armor was heaped against great bronze cannons.

Indeed, though the treasure rooms were full, the Moonrat still wanted more. He wanted as many diamonds as there were stars in the sky. He wanted dark silks as rippled with silver as the sea.

Above all, he wanted a prize no pirate had ever taken. He wanted the shining treasure he saw each night, sailing out of the sea and across the darkened sky – the treasure that was out of reach even from the highest island.

He wanted the Moon itself!

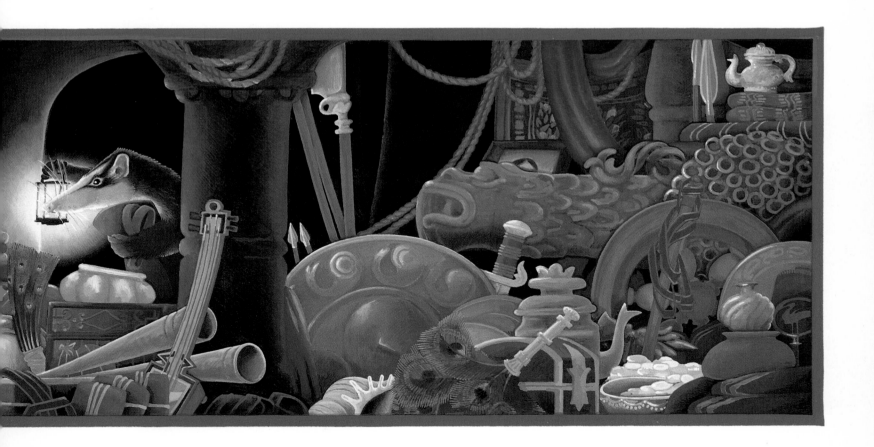

One summer brought nothing to the islands but a vicious sun. The merchant ships had grown wary of the pirate-haunted sea. Not a single masthead broke the hard, blue line of the horizon. Hot and bored, the pirates gambled with their stolen coins and quarreled among themselves.

At last, one morning a seagull lookout flew over the palace and screeched, "A ship! A ship!" The pirates clattered eagerly down the stone steps, swarmed onto the *Sea Serpent*, and headed out to sea.

Hiding in the shelter of a little island, lurking among the rocks and under canopies of hanging vegetation, the pirate ship waited in ambush. But when the quarry came in sight, the pirates cursed beneath their breath. It was a small ship, almost too small and too shabby to bother with. Still, the pirates set after it.

With sails full, the *Sea Serpent* raced after the boat and soon pulled alongside. The pirates snarled and shouted ferociously. They drummed on their shields and fired their cannons. But nobody ran on deck to surrender. There was no one aboard to frighten and worst of all . . . no treasure!

The ship's hold was empty but for a few sacks of grain. Even the captain's cabin was bare of treasure – but pinned to the walls and curled on the floor were hundreds of maps and charts.

As the Moonrat searched among them, he forgot his hunt for gold and silver. He was fascinated by the strange maps, the outlines and names of mysterious lands and unknown seas. Hastily he loaded them onto the *Sea Serpent*.

"Cut loose!" he ordered. "Set sail for home!"

Back at the hideout, the Moonrat piled the stolen maps into his room and locked his door. For days and nights, no sound was heard from within but the rolling and crackling of ancient paper and the quiet hiss of lamps.

At last, one morning the Moonrat strode out onto the palace steps and unrolled an old and dirty map before his breathless crew.

"Here is the map we have been looking for," he declared. "Here is the map to the Moon itself!"

The pirates gasped. In one curled corner of the map, beyond the warnings of sea monsters and whirlpools, was a cluster of wrecks and a small white circle with the word "*Moonrise*" written beneath it.

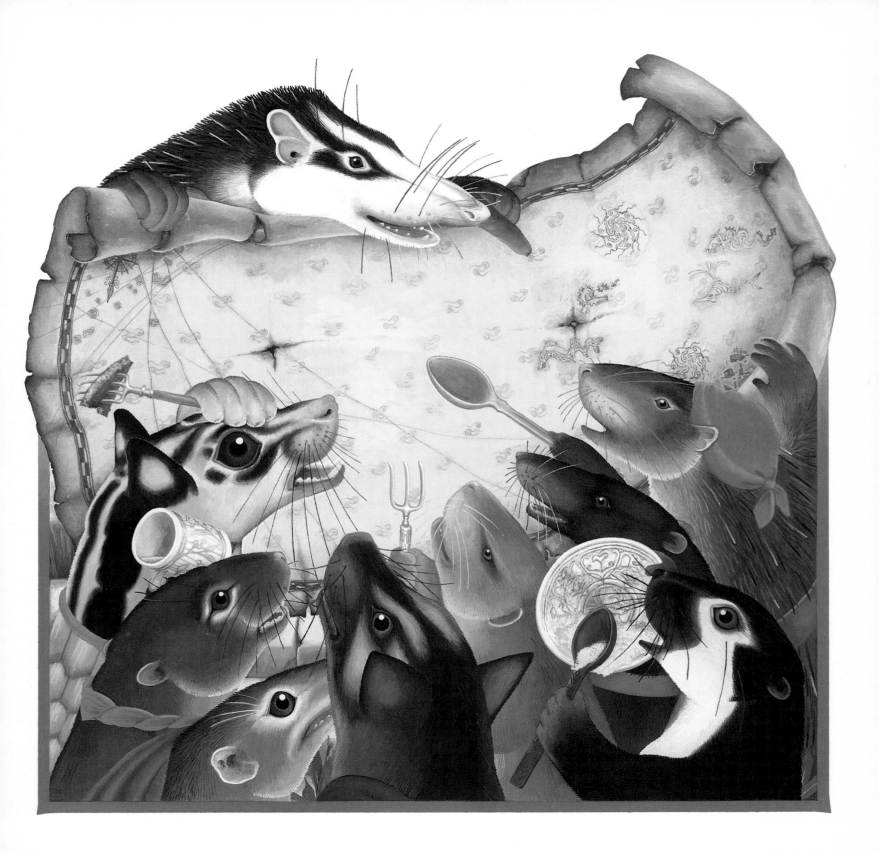

The pirates shivered with excitement and anticipation. At the Moonrat's command, they scattered to prepare the ship for a long sea voyage.

The gangplanks creaked ominously with every sack, basket, and bundle carried on board. Stores of food and fresh water were loaded. Ropes, lines and nets, and gaffs and hooks were stowed. By the time they had finished, the *Sea Serpent* sat dangerously low in the water. But the sun was high and the wind was right, so before long they had pulled the ship over the harbor floor and set sail.

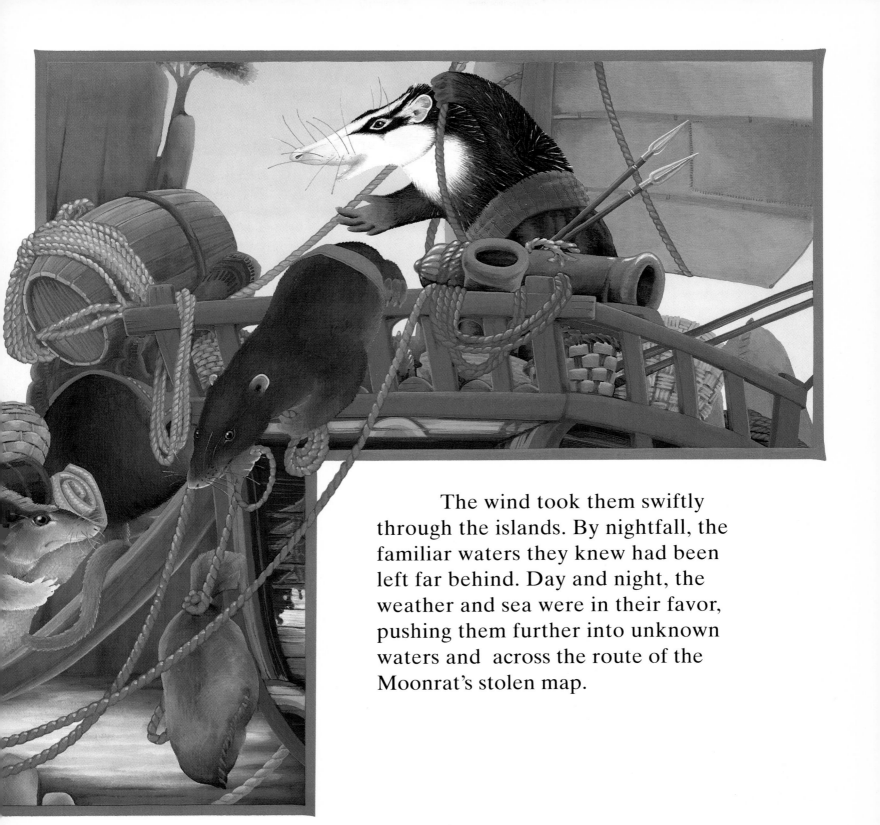

The wind took them swiftly through the islands. By nightfall, the familiar waters they knew had been left far behind. Day and night, the weather and sea were in their favor, pushing them further into unknown waters and across the route of the Moonrat's stolen map.

Suddenly, the
wind deserted them,
the sails emptied, and the
ship sat still under a hot and heavy
sky. The pirates cursed each other. They
cursed the wind. They cursed the ship. The seabirds
disappeared along with the ship's silver wake and
within days their supplies of fresh water ran low.

By night a ghostly, mournful singing rang
around and through the ship. Unseen creatures
thumped against the hull. The sky became covered
with thick clouds. The occasional ragged hole in
them revealed the stars as far away as ever, but no
sign of the Moon.

By morning the clouds would be gone and a
fierce, hot sun would bake them again. The deck
turned white and creaked painfully until buckets of

water were cast over the planking. Tiny flying fish splattered past in huge schools, terrified out of the water by unseen predators. None of the pirates dared look too closely into that dark, dense sea . . .

One morning, the night clouds remained and hid the sun. A current gripped the keel and pulled the ship onward. A dense, damp fog descended and hid the bow from the stern and one miserable pirate from the next! Water dripped from the ends of ropes and the tips of whiskers and tails. And for endless days and nights the *Sea Serpent* sailed blindly on through the cold mists.

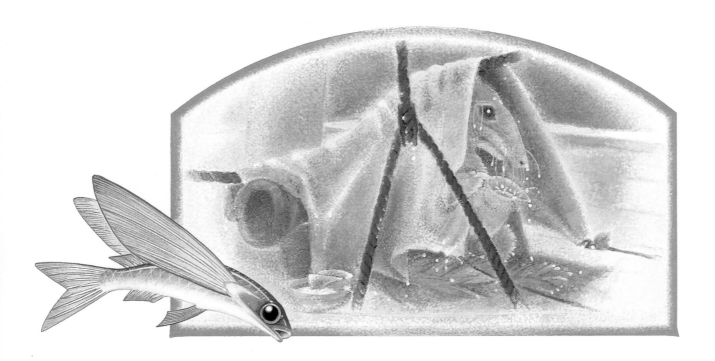

Then one day it seemed that their troubles were over. The sun rose and the fog lifted to reveal an unknown ocean. Before them lay a flat, shallow sea-graveyard. Foundered on sandbanks were centuries of sorry ships that had met their end. Tattered flags flapped carelessly from the mastheads of sunken windjammers. Down in the clear water, great shoals of silver fish swam among the spars and rigging of the wrecks. Treasure littered the sparkling white sand of the sea floor. It looked so close that they had only to reach down ... but ugly gray fish patrolled the drowned holds.

Here was the cluster of wrecks they had been looking for. They had reached their destination! This was the Moonrise Sea – the sea on the edge of the map and at the edge of the world!

The pirates sailed on until the sun set behind them and the first bright stars of the night shone above. With one last look at his map, the Moonrat ordered the nets to be pitched overboard and the rowboats launched to stretch them out across the black water.

Seated at their oars, ears twitching, noses drinking in the salty smells of an unknown sea, the pirates lay in ambush for the Moon. Sure enough, as they peered into the water they could see something round and white rising toward them out of the depths of the sea.

With a tug and a surge, the nets entrapped something large and strong. The little rowboats rocked dangerously. The pirates had to take tight hold of the ropes with teeth and claws to keep from losing their catch. The *Sea Serpent* listed wildly as the heavy nets were hauled aboard.

"The Moon! The Moon!" shrieked the Moonrat, brandishing his cutlass and gnashing his teeth with a desperate joy. And certainly the haul of glistening silver, as it lay among the nets on the deck, gleamed with all the brilliance he could have hoped for. Perhaps it was not quite as round as he had supposed, and those four flippers were quite unexpected; but it had risen at the hour of moonrise and what else could it be but the Moon?

"Hoist sail and let's away out of this forsaken ocean!" squealed the Moonrat. "Set a course for home – I'll not rest easy till this great treasure is safely hidden away!"

Again clouds covered the night sky as the *Sea Serpent* began its long journey home. And on its deck, huge and round as the Moon, pale and gleaming as the Moon, shimmering silver as water trickled off his back, lay a great and ancient White Turtle. Oldest and wisest of all sea creatures, he lay stranded now on his back, a prisoner to pirates.

"I am *not* the Moon! I am *not* the Moon!" he cried, but his language was foreign and his accent strange. And with every cry, he grew weaker. Large wet tears as salty as the sea fell from his dark eyes. He longed to be back in the deep, cool waters where he belonged, but only his tears splashed into the sea. He sighed like the wind in the wave tops, but no pirate listened. They were too busy launching the little rowboats to pull the *Sea Serpent* out of the Moonrise Sea.

"Row harder!" cried the Moonrat. But the more they heaved on the oars, the more the ship seemed held in the water. The waves rattled strangely against the ship's bow. Puzzled, the Moonrat leaned out to peer into the sea – and drew back, howling in horror!

The water beneath him was a mass of shimmering, shifting sea creatures. Under the ship, the water boiled with scaly, angry animals, each one pressing hard against the planking of the *Sea Serpent*. There were jellyfish and eels, sharks and seals, and sharp-toothed barracuda. The cries of the great White Turtle had not gone unheard after all.

Whales rolled up from the deep and showered the ship and its crew with cold sea water. It chilled the trembling pirates but cooled and comforted the sad White Turtle.

The *Sea Serpent* strained and creaked, and the mournful song that had haunted the ship before once again echoed about the hull.

With a splintering groan, the *Sea Serpent* split apart – crushed from stem to stern, like a toy boat made of matchsticks. Huge waves rolled over the broken decks as the White Turtle slipped silently back into the ocean.

The pirates swam for their lives toward the little rowboats. Large-mouthed fish nipped their toes. Crabs and shellfish clipped their trailing tails. Tossed and drenched, they struggled aboard and started to row across the seething ocean. Day and night they rowed, without food or water or sleep. At last, too tired to row, they drifted. Soon they floated into seas they would have recognized had they looked, but their eyes were still closed tight in terror.

With a grinding crunch the boats ran onto dry land. Onto a beach – a beach between two rocky towers! Their own beach! The pirates tumbled out of the boats and rolled joyfully in the sand. They hugged each familiar rock and boulder, thankful for their safe return.

That night, comfortable and well-fed, the pirates were plotting and planning once more. But then the Moon rose out of the easterly sea and sailed up into the night sky – a round, white, gleaming treasure that set the whole sea glinting. A shiver ran down each pirate's spine and they all crept quietly to bed.

Behind them, steeped in a pool of silvery light, the Moonrat vowed never again to hunt the Moon. It could stay where it belonged, sailing its course among the stars. His promise made, the Moonrat, too, went to bed and quietly slept.

And below the palace, below the rocky
towers, like a reflection of the Moon in the dark,
dark water, the great White Turtle swam on . . .
through the sea . . . and into the Moonrat's dreams.